Double Trouble

Mr. Clark looked straight at Tommy. "Would you please hand me the note, Tommy?" he asked.

"Mr. Clark, I don't think the class would be interested," said Tommy quickly, scrunching up the note. Howard leaned over and nudged Tommy. "Eat the note."

Tommy smiled and lifted the note to put it into his mouth. But Mr. Clark picked the note out of his hand and opened it up. " 'Dear Tommy, it is known that Terri R. likes you. Do you like her? Please nod your head once if you do, and twice if you don't.' "

Terri glanced around the room, looking for a guilty face. Celia Forester smirked at her. Of course, it had to be her. But how could Terri prove it? Only she and her friends knew that Celia would like to get her hands on Tommy and wanted Terri out of the way. How could she show up that impossible Celia Forester once and for all?

#4 Terri the Great

by
Susan Smith

A MINSTREL® BOOK

PUBLISHED BY POCKET BOOKS

New York   London   Toronto   Sydney   Tokyo   Singapore

A MINSTREL PAPERBACK *ORIGINAL*

A Minstrel Book published by
POCKET BOOKS, a division of Simon & Schuster
1230 Avenue of the Americas, New York, NY 10020

ISBN: 0-671-73728-7

First Minstrel Books printing January 1989

10 9 8 7 6 5 4 3 2

A MINSTREL BOOK and colophon are registered trademarks
of Simon & Schuster

Printed in the U.S.A.

For my dear friend, Josey,
with love

#4 Terri the Great

Chapter One

❀

"Yahoo!" Terri Rivera cried as she whooshed down the ski slope past a couple of her classmates.

They were all on the Gladstone Elementary School sixth-grade snow trip and were among the few kids who knew how to ski. The others were near the bottom of the mountain, taking lessons or tobogganing.

Just then, out of the corner of her eye, Terri spotted Celia Forester approaching on her left. Celia was the prettiest and most conceited girl in the sixth grade. She wasn't popular with the girls because she was so stuck up, but, of course, the boys noticed her looks. Which is a crime, Terri thought. She didn't like anything about Celia.

Celia was wearing a pink snowsuit with fake fur trim, and a pink fluffy hat. Everything about Celia was pink and fluffy, Terri decided.

"Do you want to race or do you just want to talk to me?" Terri shouted, tossing her short dark hair.

1

Even Celia knew a challenge when she heard it. "Let's race," she yelled back. "Ready, set . . . go!"

The two girls shot forward. Terri looked to her left and saw Celia flying down the slope, picking up as much speed as possible. Terri had to grudgingly admire her control.

Terri was determined to beat Celia. The cold air stung her face as she skied faster than she ever had before. Her gymnastics experience had paid off. She was limber and her legs were very strong.

Terri made quick, even turns as she zoomed next to Celia. But Celia was a gymnast, too, and Terri knew she'd be hard to beat. Celia was pretty good at it, and both of them were part of the Gladstone gymnastic team for the upcoming county-wide competition. Terry wanted to be a great gymnast and maybe go on to the Olympics someday.

Suddenly the ski shack and lift stations came into view below. Terri sped up even more and zipped past Celia. As she neared the ski lifts a ski's length ahead of Celia, everyone was cheering and clapping.

To stop, Terri made a wide turn and came to a stop in front of her three best friends, Dawn Selby, Angela King, and Sonya Plummer. The three girls slapped the snow from their suits and hobbled up to Terri in their heavy boots.

"Wow, you really showed Celia," Angela shouted excitedly, yanking off her hat so that her dark curls tumbled loose.

Just then Celia skied over to Terri. "That wasn't fair, Terri. I gave you a head start. You never told me you could really ski."

"You never asked, Celia," Terri said, grinning. "And

what's this about a head start? Get real, Forester. You'd never give anyone a break!''

"Yeah!'' Angela chimed in, waving her cap at Celia.

It was true. Only Sonya, who used to be friends with Celia, said Celia could be nice once in a while, but Terri had never experienced it. She thought that the day Celia was nice to somebody, everyone had better watch out. She had to be up to something.

"You just wait till the gymnastics competition,'' Celia said, turning on her skis.

"Oh, goody, goody. I can't wait,'' Terri replied, clapping her hands like a two-year-old. Her friends laughed. Celia skied over to her own friends, Polly Clinker and Jeannie Sandlin.

"I wonder what she's planning?'' Dawn asked, worried for her friend. The smallest of all the four, Dawn had always been thought of as the baby of the group. But since she had been elected class treasurer and solved two big mysteries her friends and family looked at her with new respect.

"Who cares? She's not as good as me,'' Terri said confidently.

"That's for sure,'' said Sonya loyally. "She's definitely not dedicated like you, Terri.''

Terri didn't want to admit it, but she was a tiny bit worried about Celia. Just the other day she heard their coach telling Celia how good she was becoming. Terri never bothered her friends with it because she didn't want them to worry. Besides, she told herself, what was there to worry about? She had won prizes for gymnastics. Celia hadn't.

Terri was good and someday she'd be the very best—the greatest!

"Let's get something to eat," Terri said, unsnapping her bindings and lifting her skis to her shoulder.

The four trooped off to the lodge, where Sonya paused in front of the plate-glass window to check herself out.

"Come on," said Terri. "This is no fashion show."

"It's important to look good at ski lodges," insisted Sonya, straightening her ponytail and smiling at her reflection.

If Sonya had a fault, it was that she was too concerned with how she looked, Terri thought. But she forgave her because she was their official fashion consultant and offered lots of good advice.

Inside the lodge, Terri spotted her parents and her three-year-old sister, Lia, standing together near the far wall.

That day was one of those rare days when Terri's parents were able to do something with her. Lately, they had both been too busy. Their work and Lia took up most of their lives and, although Terri wouldn't admit it to anyone, she was feeling jealous.

Her father, a tall, burly man with a salt-and-pepper beard, smiled as Terri approached and wrapped an arm around her shoulder. Mrs. Rivera was small and quick, with long black hair that reached almost to her waist even when tied back. They both wore jeans and looked a little like leftover hippies, which is what they used to be. When she wasn't wearing sweats, Terri dressed very conservatively.

"Guess what? I just won a race," Terri declared.

"That's great, honey," said Mrs. Rivera. "Hi, kids," she said to the others.

"Wonderful, Terri," her father said, patting her affectionately. Lia tugged at his shirttail and he dropped his arm to his side. "I wish I'd been out there watching you," he added distractedly.

Mrs. Rivera picked Lia up, and Terry's parents both smiled and cuddled the little girl.

Terri felt annoyed that they were paying attention to Lia instead of her at a time like this. After all, this was a big moment for her. "Don't you care?" she asked them suddenly.

Her parents blinked at her as though they were surprised.

"Of course, we care. We're really excited," her mother replied. "You know how excited I get about races. I'm dying to know all about it." Mrs. Rivera had been the star on the ski team at her college.

"It's fantastic. You haven't been skiing for a year and you win a race, that's great," Mr. Rivera exclaimed. "How far did you race?"

"Just down the whole side of this mountain," Terri replied proudly.

"Who were you racing against?" her mother asked, handing Lia to her husband.

"Celia Forester. The most horrible girl in the world," Terri announced dramatically.

"Terri, that's not very kind," her father said. Mr. and Mrs. Rivera exchanged glances.

"It's not supposed to be," Terri answered. "No one likes Celia Forester."

Sonya nudged Terri and pointed to the fireplace where Tommy Atwood, the cutest boy in the sixth grade, was drinking a cup of hot chocolate with Celia. They were staring into each other's eyes.

"Somebody loves her," Sonya said, giggling.

Terri narrowed her eyes when she saw Celia. Lately, Sonya had been interested in boys, but Terri still thought liking boys was dumb. Most boys were scared of her anyway, because she was such a good athlete and could beat them at almost anything. They didn't like competing against her.

"How do you know he loves her, Sonya? How do you know she's not just trying to hypnotize him?"

Dawn, Angela, and Sonya burst out laughing. Terri grinned. Celia turned to see what the commotion was about.

"She's a human being and should be treated like one," Mrs. Rivera reminded Terri.

Terri rolled her eyes. "She's just barely human, Mom. You don't know Celia. Not everyone is wonderful, you know."

Terri loved her parents, but sometimes they drove her crazy because they were so loving and caring and good about *everything*. That was one way in which Terri and her parents were not alike.

"I know that," said Mrs. Rivera, beaming at her daughter and giving her a quick squeeze. "Anyway, congratulations on the race. Obviously, you were the best skier."

Terri smiled at the praise. It seemed as if lately she couldn't get enough praise.

"Come on, squirt." Terri scooped up Lia and took her outside to play in the snow.

A few minutes later Celia sauntered out of the lodge and straight up to Lia. "Hey, baby, what's your name?"

"Lia," said Lia plainly.

"She knows her name!" Celia cried.

"She's not a peabrain, and she's not a baby," Terri scoffed.

"She's so cute," said Celia.

"It runs in the family," Terri answered.

"You wish," Celia said.

Terri packed snow into a ball and gave it to Lia. Then she made one for herself.

"Here, do this," Terri said, throwing the ball at Lia's tummy. The little girl laughed and could only toss her snowball onto the ground. Terri made her another one.

"Show Celia how cute you can be." Terri pointed Lia's hand in the direction of Celia. Lia threw the snowball right at Celia. It hit her in the knee.

"Real cute, Terri," Celia said, quickly forming a snowball and tossing it at Terri.

But Terri was quick and dodged the icy ball. Lia laughed and clapped her mittened hands.

Celia laughed at the baby. "Too bad your sister's so much cuter than you, Terri," she said, grinning.

Terri had been making a really hard snowball and let it fly at Celia with all her might. Celia was quick, too, and the snow only hit her shoulder.

At that moment Dawn and Sonya strolled out of the lodge and saw Celia wagging her finger at Terri.

"You're so immature, Terri," Celia cried and flounced off to look for her own friends.

"Celia's such a pain," Terri said, watching her walk

away as if she were a movie star. Her long red hair swayed and glistened in the sunlight.

"She's mean and she's mad because she lost the race," Sonya said, patting Terri's shoulder. "You know she can't stand to lose anything."

"Well, I can't stand to lose, either," said Terri. "And I can be just as mean as her."

"But you don't want to be mean," cried Dawn. "You just want to be the best. And we all want to be visible in a *good* way. Right, everybody?" she yelled as if she were leading a cheer.

"Right!" the other girls chorused.

The girls had formed so many clubs over the years that Terri forgot for a minute that they had started the High Visibility Club. As members they had to do something that was very visible and show everyone how great they were.

"Well, the High Visibility Club fits in perfectly with my plans," said Terri. "Everyone's going to notice me in the Gladstone County Gymnastics Competition."

"Right!" her friends shouted.

Lia clapped, too, and threw a handful of soft snow at Terri. Terri laughed, thinking of Celia's comment about Lia being cuter than her. Of course, it wasn't true. Besides, Terri had beaten Celia, which was the important thing.

But knowing how much Celia hated to lose, Terri had a feeling that Celia would try to get back at her somehow. She knew she'd have to watch out.

Chapter Two

At school on Monday everybody was standing around at their lockers and talking about the snow trip.

Linda Carmichael, a new friend of the group, was waiting for Terri, Dawn, Sonya, and Angela. Linda didn't get to go on the snow trip because she had been in some trouble just before the trip. She was very quiet while the other kids were talking.

"I wish you'd stop talking about the trip," Linda said finally. "I feel so left out."

"Sorry. I forgot," said Dawn. "What did you do while we were all gone?"

Linda shrugged. "Not much. I read a book. Went to the mall. Nothing as exciting as skiing."

"Oh, Linda, remember practice after school. Ms. Ford is going to tell us all about the competition," said Terri, pitching her social studies book into her locker. She suddenly caught a whiff of her gym clothes, which had been in the locker for much too long. "Whew!" she cried, holding her nose.

Dawn laughed. "I bet that's the world's stinkiest locker."

"Yeah," said Angela. "All your books are going to smell like dirty feet."

"Okay, okay." Terri sighed. "I'll take my gym clothes home tonight."

On the way into class, Tommy Atwood ran up to Terri. "Hey! That was some race you had with Celia," he said.

"You saw it?" she said, staring into his brown eyes. "Yeah. It was good, wasn't it?"

He nodded. "Yeah. Well, see you in class." Tommy strolled over to his seat and sat down.

Terri's friends who had piled up just behind her were giggling now. She started to tell them what Tommy had said.

"He likes you," Sonya interrupted. "Boys don't talk to girls unless they have a good reason."

Terri gave her a funny look. "Well, he had a good reason."

Terri had been in gymnastics classes with Tommy for a few years, but she hadn't ever noticed him very much. In fact, she didn't notice boys very much at all. Her friends thought Tommy was the cutest boy in the sixth grade. And now when she thought about it, Terri had to admit that he was.

After school the gymnastics team met to practice and discuss the competition. Celia was there, dressed in a hot-pink-striped leotard and matching hot-pink tights.

Linda nudged Terri. "I'll bet her gym clothes never smell."

"She's not human, remember?" Terri said, and they both giggled.

Terri glanced around the gym and noticed Howard Tarter, the funniest boy in the sixth grade, and Tommy Atwood. They were fooling around on one of the mats with some other boys.

"Girls and boys," Ms. Ford, the instructor, began in a loud voice. Everyone came to attention. Even Howard and Tommy untangled themselves from a pile-up of boys. "You may be interested to know that I've just learned that a talent scout will be coming to the competition to seek out new talent for a TV show about gymnastics. So, that may be even more reason to do your very best in the competition."

"TV," whispered Terri. She closed her eyes and imagined herself on TV with everyone she knew watching her. Of course, she wouldn't be the first student from Gladstone to be on TV. Celia Forester and her older sister had been on TV. But they had been in commercials, not on an actual show.

Even though Terri's mother made films, Terri had never been in one because they were documentaries, usually about saving wildlife or some other cause.

Terri knew she absolutely had to be on TV and she had to beat Celia in the gymnastics competition.

"I wouldn't want to be on TV," said Linda. "Somebody from one of my old schools might recognize me."

Terri looked at her as if she had grown two heads. "You've got to be the only person I've ever known who doesn't want to be on TV."

Linda shrugged. "I like to keep a low profile."

Terri forgot for a minute that Linda and her family had not lived the most perfect of lives. Now the whole family were trying to become good citizens.

"Now, let's talk about the competition itself, so that we can start to prepare for it," Ms. Ford went on. "It's a real competition. You will start with compulsories in four events. Compulsories are routines made up by the United States Gymnastics Federation. Then after compulsories you go on to the optionals—your own routines with your own tricks."

Terri had been in a lot of competitions so she knew all that, but there were a few kids on this team, like Linda, who hadn't done any competing before.

"The girls will start with vaulting, then go on to uneven parallel bars, balance beam, and floor exercises," Ms. Ford said. "You are allowed two vaults. The score of the higher one will be counted. That's how it'll be with the other competitions, too. Two tries—the better one counts. So, you *are* a team, but you are judged by your individual performances. Any questions?"

Howard raised his hand. "Do we do anything different because we're boys?"

"Good question. I hadn't gotten to the boys yet," Ms. Ford said and then explained what the boys would do that was different from the girls.

Ms. Ford put on a stern face. "So, now let's get to work."

They did their warm-up exercises first. Then the students practiced whatever they most needed help with. Terri chose the floor exercises because it took most of her energy and she liked to do it while she was fresh.

The tumbling mat was just under forty feet square, and

Terri knew she had to do a lot of fast tumbling and use up as much of the mat as possible. She mentally ran through her routine before practicing it on the mat. First the hand-springs, then the aerials, or a flip in the air without her hands touching the floor. Next a whip back, a quick back handspring without touching the floor with her hands. And finally a back tuck. Remember to keep your knees tucked up tight against your chest when you flip over, Terri reminded herself. Then came the hard part, executing it on the floor.

Celia worked on tumbling, too. Terri paused to watch her for a minute. She was small and delicate. She didn't do anything adventuresome or unusual, but she looked good because she was so graceful. Terri saw Tommy smiling at Celia when she finished an aerial.

Terri felt suddenly annoyed. Why was Tommy watching *her?* What was so great about Celia?

"Terri? Your turn on the beam," Ms. Ford said.

Terri felt as if there were a Mexican jumping bean hopping around inside her. She knew that she couldn't perform until it settled down.

She shook her hands out, took a deep breath and slowly released it. Then she began gripping the beam hard with her toes. She raised her arms and started her turn.

Turn everything at once. That's right, she coached herself. The faces of her friends whirled by in a perfect arc until she was upright again.

"Good, good, good!" Ms. Ford praised her loudly. "Perfect, Terri. Do another, and let's all watch carefully."

Terri did another turn which she thought was even better than the first. Then the other students copied her.

After class, Tommy came over to where Terri was standing. "Well, congratulations, Ms. Perfect Turn," he said.

"Thanks. You did pretty well yourself," she told him.

He shrugged. "What do you like best?"

"Tumbling," Terri told him. "It takes the most energy."

"Oh," Tommy said. "Well, you've got plenty of that." The other students were leaving the gym and their good-byes echoed in the big, empty room.

"There's a gymnastics class I'm going to see on Saturday," he told her. "They're getting ready for a competition in another state. I thought maybe you'd want to know about it, so you could go watch."

Terri felt her stomach do a somersault. "Do I? I mean, yeah, sure," she blurted out.

"Okay, I guess I'll call and tell you where it is," Tommy said, his ears growing red. "Well, see ya!"

"See ya," Terri replied. Twice in one day! She couldn't believe that Tommy had actually congratulated her twice in one day. Most boys didn't want anything to do with her!

She couldn't wait to tell her friends. Linda was there, of course, but Terri wanted to tell the others at the same time. Something this important had to be shared equally among them.

Linda did become curious. "What were you talking to Tommy about?" she asked.

"Tell you later," Terri said, slinging her gym bag over her shoulder. "Come on, let's go change."

Chapter Three

⊞

"I just knew you'd be having Rice Pops for breakfast," said Mrs. Rivera when she came to join her family at the breakfast table Tuesday morning.

"How'd you know?" Terri asked.

"I dreamed it," replied her mother. "I dreamed that Josephine Riley was making a crab salad for dinner the other night, and that's exactly what she served for dinner! I could even name the ingredients before we arrived at their house. This has been happening so often lately that I'm starting to think I'm telepathic."

Mr. Rivera buttered the toast that had just popped. "This means that I don't have to listen to the weather report anymore. I can just ask your mother whether or not it will rain."

Mrs. Rivera batted her husband playfully with a dishtowel.

"What's this all about, Mom?" Terri asked her.

"I just got a grant from the Gladstone Arts Foundation to do a documentary film on the psychic world. It'll be called *Sixth Sense—What About the Future?* and it'll be about people who make their living predicting the future, and about those who depend on their predictions. It'll cover what to watch out for when consulting a psychic or other fortune teller and how to tell a good one from a bad one. I'm going to interview people from all over. And, as usual, I'm really getting into my research," she added.

"Do you know if I'm going to win anything in the competition, Mom?" Terri asked her.

Her mother laughed. "I don't know yet. But maybe we'll find out on Saturday."

"Saturday?" Terri said. Her parents exchanged knowing looks. Mr. Rivera picked up Lia and put her into her high chair.

"We're all going to a psychic, camera crew and everybody, so keep Saturday open," said Mrs. Rivera. "I want our whole family to go because I want to have personal experience on camera."

"Oh, no," groaned Terri. "I want to be a star, but not like this!"

"It'll be exciting. You'll see," said Mrs. Rivera.

About as exciting as going to an acupuncturist, thought Terri. Her parents were always coming up with some kooky and far-out thing like this. Earlier that year, Mrs. Rivera had done a film on baby food and the whole family was enlisted to try the various brands. Then Mr. Rivera decided to create a sculpture out of the baby food jars. It was just like them, Terri thought. With every project her parents became totally involved in their work.

As producer-director of her films, Mrs. Rivera did all her own interviews, wrote the scripts, and put the films together herself. She was an independent filmmaker. Mr. Rivera worked at home as an artist. But lately, he had been doing art shows out of town, so he wasn't around as much as usual. Sometimes Terri wished she had normal parents who had normal jobs.

"Well, I don't see how a psychic can help me any," said Terri. "I already plan to have a great future."

"That's the right spirit," said Mr. Rivera, chuckling. "But maybe the psychic can tell you what you'll be eating for breakfast when you're twenty."

They all laughed. Terri finished her cereal and picked up her backpack. "Hey, I've got an idea. Try to think about what questions I'll be asked on my science test tomorrow, Mom," she said as she went out the kitchen door.

Her parents laughed and said goodbye. Terri wheeled her bike out of the garage and rode over to Dawn's to meet her friends. She hadn't had a chance to call them the night before because she'd gone out to dinner with her family. "I have something extremely important to tell you." She waited until they all gasped and asked, "What?"

"Tommy asked me to watch gymnastics class."

"Wow, is that romantic," Angela said.

"Whew! The suspense was killing me," exclaimed Linda.

"We're not exactly going there together," said Terri. "I mean, he just thought I'd like to know about it. He's going."

"Is it really an invitation?" Dawn asked. "I mean, he'll probably meet you there."

"Then it's a date," said Sonya.

"He's going to call me and let me know where it is and everything," said Terri.

"Wow, that *is* romantic," said Angela. "A boy's going to call you for something other than homework."

"Yeah. I think that's the first time in our history that this has ever happened," said Dawn. "We must be getting more mature."

For a change, Terri rode beside her friends. Usually, she rode way ahead of them, because they were slow and liked to talk, and she liked to race. Terri always tried to outdo herself.

"It's different with Tommy and me," said Terri importantly. "We have something in common. Sort of a professional relationship. I don't think of it as a romance exactly."

"Yeah? It sounds a lot like Maureen Montclair and Bryan Woodcliff," said Sonya dreamily. Those were two characters in the girls' favorite soap opera, "Maureen Montclair."

"Yeah, Maureen and Bryan are in the school play right now," said Angela. "But that's a real romance. You can tell."

"Oh, remember when Tommy had to kiss Celia in the school play?" cried Dawn.

"Who wants to remember that?" Terri demanded, leaning over her handlebars and riding far ahead of the others.

At school, Terri wanted to meet Tommy in the hall, but she didn't see him. She saw him in classes, but he only looked at her one time. He did smile, though.

She usually thought about gymnastics all the time. When she sat in math class, she imagined doing tricks on a parallelogram or a triangle. Or she imagined herself tumbling and doing tricks she didn't know how to do yet.

But she wasn't really concentrating on gymnastics that day. She kept thinking about Tommy—but she didn't know why. Maybe because other boys never talked to her—other than Howard Tarter, who was nice to everyone. In her new daydreams, Tommy was telling her how great she was. She decided she liked hearing him say that.

After school, Sonya waited outside for Terri. "Want to go get a soda?" she asked.

"No, thanks. I have a gym practice, and then I want to go straight home and study," said Terri. Actually, she wanted to go straight home in case Tommy called.

Running through the door, she heard the phone and snatched it up. "Hello," she said, trying not to pant.

It was Tommy. "Hi. How are you?" he asked.

"Just fine," Terri said, still breathless.

"I wanted to let you know that the gym class is on Saturday at ten o'clock, at the Winchell Auditorium. Can you make it?"

"Saturday?" Then Terri remembered. Her heart sank to her shoes. "Ah," she stalled, then told the truth. "I'm supposed to go somewhere with my parents that morning. But maybe I can get out of it," she added quickly. "I'd rather go to the class. I mean, it's my future . . . and everything."

"Well, if you go, I'll see you there," said Tommy after clearing his throat. "And if you don't go, I won't see you."

"Yeah, I guess not," said Terri, more disappointed than she wanted to be. She didn't want him to know, though.

"It's too bad. If you don't get to go, that is," Tommy went on nervously. "You'd probably like it. I saw them last year and they were great."

"Sure, well, I'll talk to my parents," Terri told him, and then they said goodbye.

She closed her eyes and wished she could get her parents to say yes just by thinking about it.

"No, I'm sorry, Terri," said Mr. Rivera. "We told you all about it this morning. It's important to us as a family and for the film."

"But, Dad! This is important to my career as a gymnast!" Terri insisted. "You know how important it is to me."

"But you can go watch this class anytime," her mother said. "And, remember, we made these plans to do something as a family. I want this film to have a family angle because this psychic specializes in doing families. She gets amazing vibrations from whole families."

"Can't you borrow some other family?" Terri persisted.

"No, I want ours," Mrs. Rivera replied firmly.

"You're ruining my life!" Terri shouted, and ran off to her room and slammed the door.

Her parents came to the door and knocked. "Go away. I don't want to talk to you right now," she told them. She turned on a record album, one which she used for tumbling, and she practiced handstands. Whenever she was upset, she didn't cry. Instead, she exercised until she felt better.

Then she called Sonya and told her what had happened.

"Why did your parents pick Saturday for togetherness?" asked Sonya. "That's so inconvenient."

"Tell them that," grumbled Terri. "I've got to tell Tommy. D'you know his number?" Sonya knew the number because she used to be his lab partner.

"Well, maybe after you get back from the psychic we can all go to the mall or something," suggested Sonya.

"Okay. Well, I'll talk to you later." Then Terri dialed Tommy's number.

"This is Terri," she said.

"Oh, hi. How are you?" said Tommy.

Terri could hear giggling in the background. She thought he probably had a bunch of guys over at his house.

"I just called to tell you I have to go somewhere with my parents on Saturday, so I won't get to see the class. But thanks for telling me about it," she said.

"Yeah, well, you're welcome," Tommy said. It sounded like he was going to start laughing.

"Is something funny?" Terri asked.

"No, not really," Tommy replied. "It's just some friends of mine are here, and they're trying to get me to laugh—you know."

"Yeah. Okay, well, goodbye." Terri hung up and stared at her walls, which were covered with posters of gymnasts. She thought about the gym class that she wouldn't be going to. She could go the next weekend, maybe, just like her mother said. She liked Tommy, but not romantically or anything. So why was she so disappointed about not going to the Saturday class?

Chapter Four

⚘

Early Saturday morning the Riveras drove into the country to Selena Cantrero's farm. In Gladstone, the country wasn't far from town. In fact, Sonya lived on a ranch that was only ten minutes from Terri's house by bike.

Selena was the psychic. "We met her at a party," explained Mrs. Rivera. "In fact, she's the one who gave me the idea for the film. She knew things about us without our telling her."

"Like what?" Terri wanted to know.

"Like how old you and Lia are and what your personalities are like," Mrs. Rivera told her.

"How can a complete stranger know anything about us?" Terri asked. "You must've told her something."

"No, we didn't tell her much," Mr. Rivera said. "She's just very perceptive, that's all."

"Well, Mom is pretty perceptive, too," said Terri. "She can figure out breakfasts in advance."

Mrs. Rivera laughed and Lia began to squirm in her car seat. "Cookie, Mommy," she asked. Mrs. Rivera handed her back a cookie from the bag in the front seat.

Just then Mr. Rivera started down the driveway to Selena's house. There was no sign on the gate saying she was a psychic. Only "Selena Cantrero" was printed on her black mailbox in white block letters.

"I'm glad she doesn't call herself Madame Something," said Terri as they pulled up to the house. She clambered out of the car and stretched. "And I'm glad she doesn't live in a tepee," she added in a whisper.

Her parents laughed and led the way to the house. Billie Hunter, the camerawoman, was already there and waiting.

The farmhouse, painted red, was surrounded by white fences. A horse grazed near the barn and a few chickens walked around in the yard. Lia laughed and chased them.

Selena greeted the Riveras at the door. Her whole face lit up when she smiled. She had large gray eyes and gray hair cut to about half an inch all over her head. Selena might live in a normal-looking place, Terri thought, but she herself looked kind of weird. Her long denim skirt swept the floor, and her silver bracelets jingled when she moved.

"Come in!" she exclaimed, making a huge looping gesture with her arms.

They walked into the house. Terri expected that there would be beaded curtains and pots of burning incense, but it was a pretty normal house. Selena had a bunch of wooden statues of naked people in her living room, sort of like the African ones Howard Tarter had brought to class once. There were many potted plants, and all the rooms were full of light. The furniture was all normal and modern, nothing strange.

They moved on to the end of a long hall where there were two rooms connected by a door.

"You can sit in here and wait," said Selena to Mr. and Mrs. Rivera. "I'd like to talk to Terri first."

This made Terri feel special. She and Billie followed Selena into the adjacent room and closed the door. While Billie got herself set up, Selena began talking.

"Your father tells me that you have something important to ask me," Selena said, as though she already knew what the question was.

"Maybe you should tell me since you can read minds," said Terri. Billie's camera was pointed at her. She smiled.

Selena laughed. "You want to know if you're going to win your competition."

"Yeah, that's it!" Terri jumped out of her seat. "Will I win?"

"You're part of a gymnastics team," said Selena. "And your team will come away with medals. So will you."

"But will we get on TV?" Terri persisted. "A talent scout is coming to look at us."

"I do see cameras and a screen in your future, yes," Selena said with her eyes closed. "But it isn't going to happen as you think it will."

Terri wanted to jump up and pace around the room, but knew it would be rude. "What's that supposed to mean? Are you sure you're doing this right? I mean, aren't you supposed to use a crystal ball or some cards or something?"

"I don't need them," replied Selena. "I'm just open to seeing your future."

"I want to be famous someday," said Terri. "Do you see that?"

"Yes, I see that you'll be well known." Selena's eyes fluttered open and she smiled at Terri. "Work very hard, as you do now, and you'll be what you want to be."

Terri sighed heavily, but she wasn't sure she felt relieved. It felt to her as if Selena was not answering her directly.

"What else do you see? Am I going on a trip or anything? Fortune tellers always tell you you're going on a trip," said Terri, giggling.

"You just came back from one. The snow," said Selena. "You won a ski race against your enemy."

"Right," Terri said, pleased with that answer.

"*And* I see a romance in your near future, just blossoming, the petals stirring slightly now."

"Romance for me? Yuck!" cried Terri. "I have a friend, Tommy Atwood, but we're just friends. I'm sure it's not a romance. It's purely professional."

"I think not," Selena said. "You don't know yourself very well yet. Your feelings have not woken up."

Terri frowned. She turned to Billie. "Please cut all that stuff about romance." Billie nodded and smiled.

Terri decided she only liked what Selena said about the competition and the cameras.

"I guess that's all I want to know then," said Terri. "I'll send in my parents."

After her mom and dad went in, Terri decided the whole thing was a little like going to the doctor. She stayed in the outer room with Lia, and rearranged the throw rugs into tunnels so Lia could roll her toy trucks through them. When Lia got tired, she banged on the door, wanting to get into the room where her parents were.

"Come on, Lia, get away from there. They'll be out soon," said Terri, pulling at her sister's hand.

"I want Mommy and Daddy," Lia whined.

Terri put her ear to the door, just in time to hear Selena saying, "The baby will do great things. She'll be known worldwide for her talents."

"What about Terri?" Mrs. Rivera asked. "She's a gymnast, and she's already showing a lot of promise."

"Her star will burn differently," Selena explained. "She won't be like Lia."

"But you've only met Terri once, and Lia is just three years old," Mr. Rivera persisted. "You can't know our children as well as we do."

"Your knowledge of them blinds you to who they'll become in the future," said Selena.

"All right, what about my wife's telepathy?" asked Mr. Rivera. He sounded a little impatient. "Tell us about that."

Terri moved away from the door and looked at her sister. Lia handed her a truck, and Terri pushed it under the rug. Lia didn't know anything yet, Terri thought. She didn't care about greatness. What did that stupid psychic know anyway? Selena had to be a fraud.

But somehow, Selena's saying that Lia was going to be great upset Terri more than she wanted to admit—even to herself.

"You're not going to use all that stuff the psychic said in the film, are you, Mom?" Terri asked on the way home.

"No. Not all of it, of course," replied Mrs. Rivera. She was scribbling notes to herself in a small notebook. "But I thought I got some pretty good material."

Terry slouched down in her seat, feeling as if a cloud had dropped over her.

Later that day Terri met her friends to go to the mall. She was still in a bad mood and rode far ahead of the others, madly dodging potholes in the road.

"Hey, Terri, what's wrong with you?" Angela asked when she finally caught up with her.

"Nothing," Terri shot back.

"You look mad, you act mad, and you talk mad," said Angela. "Are you mad?"

"No," Terri said between gritted teeth.

Dawn rode up beside her next. "What's going on, Terri? You look like you're ready to punch somebody."

"Nothing, okay?" Terri stopped her bike and glared at her friends.

"You're acting prickly as a porcupine," said Sonya.

"Porcupines probably don't have little sisters who are going to be world famous," Terri blurted out.

"They do have relatives," said Dawn simply.

Angela looked sideways at Terri. "What do you mean, Terri? Did somebody say something about Lia being world famous?"

"No. I mean, yes. We went to that psychic this morning, remember? For my mother's film? And she said my sister was meant to do great things, and that I would be well known, but no big deal," Terri said, swallowing an unfamiliar lump in her throat.

"She didn't!" cried Sonya.

"I don't believe it, Terri!" Angela added. "*We* all know you're going to be famous."

"She said I would be, but Lia's supposed to be the really great one," Terri said.

"How can she be great?" Sonya wanted to know. "She's barely toilet trained."

"Yeah, right," said Angela.

Dawn said, "Didn't your parents tell her how good you are in gymnastics?"

"Yeah. My father said she couldn't know us as well as he and Mom do. But she said, 'Your knowledge of your children blinds you to what they will be in the future.' "

"Oh, that's crazy," Sonya said. "Your parents are really proud of you. They know you're super. They won't believe her."

Terri slowly grinned. "Yeah, I guess you're right." But she wasn't sure. "D'you know what else the psychic said? She said there was a romance in my future and *that* I know for sure she's totally wrong about!"

"Ha-ha," Sonya cried. "Maybe she is right, Terri. Tommy Atwood . . ." she said in a singsong.

"Tommy and Terri—that does sound romantic," said Dawn.

"It's not romantic at all!" Terri declared, pedaling ahead of her friends.

At the mall they locked up their bikes and went straight to Ellen's Hosiery where they were meeting Linda.

Linda was there already, looking through a rack of leotards, for the one with blue stripes that both girls needed.

When the two girls came out of the dressing room, everyone admired them.

"You're skinny as a twig," commented Sonya. "But you've got breasts!"

Terri felt her face grow hot. "Shhh!"

"Maybe you should get a bra, Terri," suggested Angela. The others giggled. The saleswoman glanced over at them.

"Well, I wear one," Sonya offered.

"I don't want one," said Terri.

"It's not fair," said Sonya. "You don't care about having breasts, and you've got enough for all of us."

"Maybe I should give transplants," said Terri.

Each girl looked at her own chest and then looked at one another. For the first time Terri noticed that her breasts had grown larger than her friends'.

"Okay, I'll get a bra," said Terri. "I've got my mom's credit card." She picked out a stretchy sports bra which wouldn't show under a leotard.

Outside the store, Dawn looked longingly at Terri's package. "I wish I'd gotten a bra. But actually I don't know why—breasts are no big deal."

Angela focused on Dawn's chest. "Well, yours aren't a big deal, anyway."

The others broke into laughter.

"Why do we want breasts?" Dawn asked.

"So boys will notice us," replied Linda.

"I want them to notice my mind," Dawn said.

Terri laughed and said teasingly, "Good luck, Pinhead." Then she looked up and was surprised to see Tommy and Howard walking toward them. "Shhh. Look who's coming."

She realized just then that the five of them were still standing outside Ellen's. Frilly undergarments were displayed in the window behind the girls.

"Hi," said Terri. "What're you guys doing here?"

Tommy grinned at her. "Going to a movie. The class was good this morning, Terri. Too bad you couldn't come."

"Yeah, well, some other time," she said. She wondered if he saw her blushing.

"What'd you buy?" asked Tommy.

"Oh, just a new leotard," replied Terri quickly, glancing at Linda.

Linda covered her mouth to keep from laughing. Howard nudged Tommy. "I bet it's underwear," he said, and Tommy laughed.

"You guys are gross," said Dawn.

Terri looked at Tommy and saw him gazing at one of the bra straps, which was sticking out of the top of her bag. Blushing, she tried to stuff it back in but her hands felt as if she had on boxing gloves. She watched in horror as the bag slipped from her grasp and fell to the floor, *both* straps now exposed. Terri grabbed the bag and shoved it under her arm.

The boys were doubled over with laughter.

"Go away!" commanded Terri, threatening to hit them with the bag.

The boys ran off, and then the girls started laughing, too.

"That had to be my most embarrassing moment," said Terri, giggling.

Chapter Five

On Monday Terri wore her new bra to school. Her mother had wanted her to get one for some time, and had enthusiastically gone out and bought her three more.

Terri found that now she couldn't stop looking at everyone's chests. Angela, Sonya, and Linda were very conscious of their chests, too. Terri remembered that the friends noticed themselves more each time anyone they knew got a bra.

Terri ran into Celia in the hall before homeroom. Celia had a big grin on her face.

"Something is definitely wrong," said Terri to her friends. "Celia's up to something."

"I don't want to know," groaned Angela. "I'm sure it's awful."

In homeroom Celia kept glancing over at Terri and grinning mysteriously. It was driving Terri crazy. Did Celia know she had bought a bra over the weekend? Was she going to be on TV or something? Did she know something nobody else knew? The suspense was awful.

Finally, after the morning announcements and the flag salute, Celia raised her hand. When Ms. Bell called on her, she stood up. "I'd just like everyone to know that I have an autograph from a real Olympic gymnast, Cassie Baumgarten. My cousin just happens to be best friends with her." She held up a card with some writing on it.

A couple of kids said "ooh" and "aahh," but Terri made a noise like she was going to throw up.

Ms. Bell gave her a sharp look. "Teresa, that's enough. Celia, perhaps you'd like to pass the autograph around so the class can see it."

Celia smirked at Terri and handed the autograph around.

Howard Tarter examined it closely, then read it aloud in a funny voice. " 'Dear Celia, Wishing you best of luck in your competition! Love, Cassie Baumgarten.' " Then he handed it to the next person. "Wow, I wish she'd written that to me," he murmured and batted his eyelashes. Everyone laughed.

Terri leaned over and whispered to Howard, "Cassie wouldn't sign the card with 'love' if she knew what Celia was really like."

After school Terri walked along behind Tommy and Celia as they all walked to the gymnasium for team practice. Terri wondered why Tommy would bother to walk with Celia.

Inside the girls' locker room, Celia sauntered up to Terri while Terri was hopping on one foot, the other stuck in her leotard.

"Too bad you missed out on Winchell Auditorium," she

said, smiling her sickening smile. "Tommy and I had so much fun."

"Oh?" Terri said, too surprised to say anything. She was still trying to shove her right leg into the suit while hopping in a circle.

"Yeah, I learned so much," she said gaily. "I'm so glad Tommy invited me."

"He invited *you?*" Terri asked in horror, finally losing her balance and falling flat on her backside.

Celia giggled, looking pleased. "Yes. I think I might go again this weekend."

For once in her life Terri couldn't think of anything to say. She just glared up at Celia and pulled her leotard on from her seat on the floor. How could Tommy invite Celia just because I couldn't go? Terri asked herself. She couldn't believe he'd like somebody as creepy as Celia enough to ask her to go to that class with him.

During practice Terri watched Tommy and decided that he didn't look as good as he used to. Celia told the whole class about her cousin and Cassie Baumgarten. Then Terri overheard her telling Ms. Ford that knowing a famous gymnast was going to help their chances in the competition.

"It will do no such thing, young lady," declared Ms. Ford. "Winning the competition has nothing to do with who you know. Performance is everything."

Terri was pleased that Ms. Ford put Celia down. But later, Celia did a series of cartwheels and handstands across the floor that had everyone clapping.

"Fantastic floor work, Celia!" cried Ms. Ford, who

never got really excited. "If you can perform like that in competition, then we've got fabulous chances."

Celia stood in front of the class next to Ms. Ford, smiling as if she had just won an Academy Award or something.

"She's sickening," groaned Linda. "I know she's good, but she gets away with murder."

"She's not that good and she can't get away with murder forever," said Terri, because she knew she would think of some way to get back at Celia.

"I thought Tommy was a different kind of person," Terri told her friends later when they were at her house. She was jumping on the trampoline and Linda was working on a balance beam Terri's Dad had made.

"Well, maybe Celia tricked him into going with her," suggested Sonya. "She's tricky."

"Yeah," agreed Dawn. "Or maybe she didn't go with him at all. She's probably making it sound like a bigger deal than it is."

"You know, maybe Celia overheard him talking about the class and invited herself."

"Yeah, that could be," replied Terri. "But if he really likes her, then he can't be a very good person."

That was always how Terri thought. She saw things in black and white. When Sonya was friendly with Celia, Terri practically disowned her.

Just then Lia darted in and smeared a peanut butter and jelly sandwich all over the side of the trampoline. Dawn picked her up.

"Lia, what're you doing in here?" yelled Terri. "You always mess things up."

Lia looked ready to cry.

"I know what you mean, Terri," said Dawn. "Tammy and Peter are always getting into everything."

"I always wished I had a brother or sister," said Sonya. "Sometimes I get lonely."

"Yeah, me, too," said Angela. "I don't always like being an only child. If there was another kid in the family, there would be somebody else for my mother to feed." Angela's mother was a food critic for a magazine.

The others laughed.

"Well, Dawn and I have the most family members," said Linda. "But mine are the most embarrassing." Some members of Linda's family had been in trouble with the law.

"At least your brothers aren't always playing practical jokes," said Dawn.

"No, they *are* practical jokes," replied Linda, laughing.

"I used to want a sister—until I got one," moaned Terri. "Now sometimes I'd like to give her back." She jumped off the trampoline and took Lia from Dawn. Then she carried her back upstairs to Hildy, the baby-sitter.

"The trouble with Lia is that she's old enough to make messes, but not old enough to pick them up," said Linda.

"I'd like to send Lia and Tommy to the same planet," Terri announced, walking back into the room a minute later. "And Celia to a different planet because I wouldn't want her to have too much fun with Tommy."

"You're in one of your mad-at-the-world moods," said

Sonya sympathetically. "Maybe we should have hot fudge sundaes."

They got out all the stuff for hot fudge sundaes. Terri imagined doing horrible things to Celia, like dropping a blob of fudge on her pretty pink pants or in her hair. Or pouring chopped nuts in her sneakers.

"Or how about dropping glue in her hair?" suggested Terri.

The others laughed.

"That sounds pretty rotten, Terri," said Sonya. "Besides, you'd have to tie her down."

Terri dropped a big spoonful of hot fudge on her ice cream. "Nothing's too rotten for Celia Forester," she said in a deadly serious voice.

Dawn's eyes grew round and huge, and the girls all looked at one another solemnly.

"Wow," they whispered and nodded.

Terri liked it when her friends agreed with her. She knew that they knew she was right.

Chapter Six

❁

On Wednesday Terri decided to ignore Tommy. If he was going to be a creep and like Celia, then she didn't want anything to do with him.

During art, Tommy came over to Terri and asked to see the potato print she was making. She plopped it down in front of him without speaking.

"Is something wrong, Terri?" he asked.

"No," she replied, keeping her eyes on the tabletop in front of her.

"What are you doing for your solo in the competition?" he asked.

"I'm working on something fast," she said, still not looking at him.

"I'm tumbling—lots of jumps," he said.

"I guess Winchell Auditorium really inspired you," said Terri. She wondered if Celia had been inspired by it, too.

"Yeah, it did. You should've come," he said.

Terri was still smarting from the fact that Celia had been there with Tommy. She still didn't know exactly what had happened, but it didn't matter. The fact was that Tommy and Celia had been together, and Terri wasn't there. That was all that mattered to her.

"You sound like you're mad or something," said Tommy.

"I always sound like this," insisted Terri. Then the bell rang.

"Well, see you," Tommy said, and walked out of the room. Terri looked up and saw that Celia had been watching her and Tommy talking.

Terri stuck her tongue out at Celia and dashed off to join her friends at lunch.

"If Celia wants something she just goes out and gets it," said Linda, picking lettuce off what everyone called "mushburgers."

"She doesn't always get what she wants," Sonya said. "But she always tries to get attention."

"We all like attention," said Dawn. "Remember, we want people to notice us. But we're going to do it right—as members of the High Visibility Club."

"Can I join?" asked Linda.

The others exchanged glances.

They couldn't forget how much trouble Linda had been in recently and wished she hadn't been visible then. So Terri finally made a joke and said, "We just got finished getting you out of trouble and making you invisible, Linda."

Linda hung her head so that her long blond hair hung

over her face. "Yeah, I know what you mean, but I've been trying."

"We know," Dawn said, putting a hand on Linda's shoulder. Dawn was Linda's best friend in Gladstone. "We're proud of you. Everybody notices how good you are."

Linda brightened. "Yeah? Well—maybe in gymnastics."

"Yeah, you are *definitely* visible in gymnastics," Terri said. "We'll *seriously* think about your membership to the club, right everybody?"

"Shhh!" someone hissed, throwing a note onto Dawn's desk. Dawn passed it to the person sitting across from her. Terri watched tensely. They were in math, and the teacher, Mr. Clark, was really mean when it came to note passing. Nobody, absolutely nobody, passed notes in that class. The reason—Mr. Clark read them aloud if he found one! He seemed to have eyes in the back of his head, so he saw everything that went on in the class.

Mr. Clark was giving a lesson at the blackboard. He turned around just at the exact moment the note landed on Tommy's desk. Tommy didn't see Mr. Clark looking at him, so he opened the note and read it. His ears turned bright red, and he looked up and glared at Terri.

She shook her head frantically. Did he think that she sent it? Why would she want to get him in trouble?

Mr. Clark looked straight at Tommy. "Would you please hand me that note, Tommy?" he asked.

"Mr. Clark, I don't think the class would be interested," said Tommy quickly, scrunching up the note.

A couple of students giggled.

"Nevertheless, you know the procedure in this class," Mr. Clark insisted.

"But it's not my fault that someone sent me this note, and it's about me!" protested Tommy. Now his face was tomato red.

"It should be a lesson, then," Mr. Clark replied stiffly.

Howard leaned over and nudged Tommy. "Eat the note."

Tommy smiled and lifted the note to put it into his mouth. But Mr. Clark plucked the note out of his hand and opened it up.

" 'Dear Tommy, It is known that Terri R. likes you. Do you like her? Please nod your head once if you do, and twice if you don't.' "

The whole class burst out laughing.

"I saw Tommy nod his head once," sang out one of the boys.

"Tommy likes Terri!" another one yelled gleefully.

Tommy looked embarrassed and furious—and he was staring straight at Terri. She could feel her face grow really hot.

She jumped up suddenly. "Mr. Clark and Tommy, I didn't know anything about the note. I think it's unfair—somebody was trying to embarrass me and Tommy! And we're friends!"

"I'm sorry this had to involve you, Terri. But rules are rules. I think the note is silly, but it says what it says," Mr. Clark answered.

"It's not fair!" Terri cried. She glanced around the room, looking for a guilty face. Celia Forester smirked at her. Of course, it had to be Celia. But how could Terri prove it? Only she and her friends knew that Celia would like to get her hands on Tommy and wanted Terri out of the way.

When class was dismissed, Tommy shot out of the room without speaking to anyone. Howard ran after him.

Terri went right over to Celia. "Now see what you did!" she cried. "He thinks *I* had something to do with it!"

Celia smiled. "Well, I didn't do anything," she said. Polly Clinker came to stand next to her.

Terri's friends walked over to back her up.

"Oh, yeah? I don't believe you. You probably forged my handwriting, too," Terri said, sticking her face right up close to Celia's.

"Ha-ha. Nobody could forge your scribble!" Celia said, laughing.

"That's not nice," Dawn cried.

"You'd better be careful what you say," warned Angela.

"Why are you sticking up for Tommy if you don't like him?" Celia chanted.

"Because he's my friend!" Terri shouted. "And what's it to you?"

"Yeah!" yelled the rest of the friends.

Celia and Polly walked away, smiling.

"They're acting like they won something," Sonya said.

"Yeah. They just won the prize for being the World's Most Disgusting People," said Terri.

"Here comes Howard," said Sonya.

"Terri, Tommy thinks you put one of your friends up to writing the note," said Howard.

Terri gasped. "Why would he think that?"

Howard shrugged. "Well, girls do that kind of stuff, you know. But, anyway, he never wants to speak to you again."

Terri felt as though she had just been punched in the stomach. She crossed her arms over her chest and said, "Well, that's just fine. Because I never want to *see* him again!"

Chapter Seven

After school Wednesday, Terri, Dawn, Angela, and Sonya were walking home through the downtown part of Gladstone. Terri spotted a sign that read: "Psychic—Readings by Madame O—$1."

"Oh, let's go in," suggested Dawn.

Terri scowled. "Not after my last experience. Psychics are frauds."

All her friends were peering in the window, trying to see through the filmy white curtains.

"You don't have to take it seriously," said Sonya.

Dawn took a collection from the others. "We have three dollars altogether," she announced.

"Come on. It'll be fun," Angela said. She was already at the door, ringing the doorbell before Terri could protest.

Usually, she was the one who told everyone else what to do. But sometimes, like now, she noticed that they went ahead and did things when they knew she didn't want to.

"Okay, okay," she said reluctantly, trailing her friends.

They were greeted at the door by a woman with a cloud of red hair, dressed in a red, blue, and white gown. She ushered them into the front parlor.

"Do you want your futures told together or separately?" Madame O asked.

"We want as many fortunes as we can buy for three dollars and twenty-five cents," said Dawn.

The woman smiled. "Well, I can do four fortunes. I'll give you a discount since you've brought me so much business."

"Discount fortunes," Terri muttered, and the others laughed. They decided to have their fortunes told together.

They sat down cross-legged in front of Madame O, and told her how many brothers and sisters they each had and what their families were like.

Then Dawn began to speak. "What I really want to know is will I win another election?"

"Yes, it looks like you will run for a higher office," Madame O said in a slow voice. "In one of your past lives, you worked in government office. But you're going to live a long life and have several careers. You will marry a childhood friend."

The girls laughed.

Terri thought she sounded like a psychic was supposed to sound—weird.

"Maybe you'll be president," Sonya said, nudging Dawn.

Dawn smiled with satisfaction.

Then Madame O said to Angela, "You have been dieting."

"Yeah, that's right!" Angela cried excitedly. "I want to know if I'll be thin forever. I lost the weight when I was auditioning for *West Side Story.*"

"Yes, I think I see a thin future for you, but you're always going to have to work at being thin," Madame O droned on.

"No pigging out, you mean," said Angela wistfully. "Ah. Too bad."

"You have great will power and determination and can do anything if you set your mind to it. I see you have great talent as an actress," Madame added.

"I do! You're right." Angela jumped up in delight. "Did you hear that, guys?"

"*We* already knew it," Terri said.

Sonya asked, "Well, am I a budding actress, too? I mean, I've been in plays and taken dancing for long enough."

She and Angela had been in *West Side Story* together.

"Yes, you are, Sonya, but you're a different kind of actress. Angela will eventually become an acupuncturist. You'll do serious drama. You're going to be a good lawyer."

"A lawyer!" exclaimed Sonya. "I never thought of being a lawyer. What's that got to do with acting?"

Everyone laughed.

Angela started clowning. "And where were *you* on the night of Friday the thirteenth? Is it true that you are madly in love with Howard Tarter?"

Sonya collapsed in giggles. "Stop! Okay, okay!"

"What about this young lady? Terri, is it?" Madame O asked. "You're awfully quiet, and I suspect you're not usually quiet at all. In another life, you were a radio announcer.''

Angela giggled. ''That sounds right. She's the noisiest one of us all!''

Terri glared at Angela, while the others laughed. ''Okay, okay. I'm just not crazy about this idea, that's all.''

''Well, you have no reason to be nervous. You're extremely talented and you're entered in a competition, is that right?'' Madame O asked.

Terri nodded. ''Yes, I am. I'm entered in the Gladstone County Gymnastics Competition.''

''You're going to be a star,'' droned on Madame O.

''Oh, my mom's film?'' Terri asked.

''No, you're not expecting this. But this competition I see in your future. There are many competitions for you,'' Madame O said. ''There is the gymnastics competition, of course. Then a competition with an enemy, and I see a tall, dark-haired boy in your life.''

''He's not in the picture anymore,'' Terri said harshly.

''He's your husband,'' said Madame O. ''And your enemy is going to move away. You work hard, and you have huge energy. Just be careful where you direct that energy.''

''Ha, that's not hard,'' Terri declared, pushing herself up from the floor. The other girls stood, and Dawn handed over the money and thanked Madame O. ''We had a nice time,'' she said.

Madame O smiled sweetly as the girls filed out to the street.

''What did you think?'' asked Dawn once they were safely outside.

''I thought she was a lot better than the last one,'' said

Terri. "Except really kooky, with all that stuff about other lives. I think I'll tell my mom to interview her for her film."

"Yeah, I'm really glad she didn't tell me I was going to die young or something," said Angela. "I mean, there was nothing bad in the fortunes at all. Nobody having an accident or anything. But some pretty dumb stuff about me becoming an acupuncturist." She picked up a twig and pretended to poke Dawn's arm. Everyone laughed.

"Stop!" cried Dawn. "You'll get plenty of practice in acupuncture college. I just wonder who the childhood friend is that I'm supposed to marry."

"Remember, that was just for fun, anyway," Sonya reminded the others. "And she only cost us three dollars and twenty-five cents."

"That's right," agreed Terri. "The one my parents took us to cost seventy-five dollars, and I didn't like what she said."

"I wonder how she knows all this stuff," Dawn said.

"She makes up most of it," said Sonya.

"She's extra sensitive," said Terri, remembering what the first psychic had told her. "She can feel who we are."

"I thought you weren't going to take any of this seriously," Angela said. "Now you sound like a psychic expert or something."

"Yeah, Terri. And you said they were all hoaxes," Sonya added.

"Well, some of them are," protested Terri. "My mom is interviewing all kinds of kooks. I wish I'd asked Madame O more about Celia."

"She's moving away," said Dawn. "What a relief."

"She was probably a walrus in her past life," said Terri, and everyone laughed.

All the girls went to Terri's house for a snack. Maybe Madame O had said some pretty crazy things about her friends, but Terri was secretly very pleased with what the psychic had said about her. It erased what the first one had said. She liked how Madame O talked about all her competitions. It made her life sound really exciting.

When her parents got home, Terri told them about the psychic and suggested her mother interview her. Mrs. Rivera added Madame O to the list of interview candidates.

Then she and Mr. Rivera began talking about going to an astrologer.

"That sounds like fun, Mr. and Mrs. Rivera," said Dawn. "I always read my horoscope in the paper."

"I thought it would be fun to have the whole family's chart drawn up for the film," explained Mrs. Rivera, looking amused.

"Maybe we'll get some advice about what day we should buy a new refrigerator," joked Mr. Rivera.

Terri rolled her eyes, then turned to her friends. "Welcome to the craziest family in the entire world."

Everyone laughed.

Chapter Eight

❁

Thursday morning Sonya arrived at school late. She walked in and stood at her locker with a veil wrapped around her head and face.

"What's with you?" asked Terri, shoving her books under her arm.

"I'm playing fortune teller," she said. "I'm Madame S."

Howard stopped and looked at her. "Who are you supposed to be? The genie from Aladdin's lamp?"

Everyone laughed.

"No, silly. I'm a psychic. Want your fortune told?" she asked, waving the end of the veil under his nose.

"What a great idea," said Howard as he started walking away. "But it'll have to be in five words or less because the bell is about to ring."

The bell rang. There was no time for a fortune. Sonya

picked up her books and got them all tangled up in the veil.

"Careful. You'll strangle yourself," warned Terri, laughing.

The girls caught up with Howard.

"Hey, why don't we tell fortunes at lunch?" suggested Howard.

"We can set up a card table and have a regular business. We'll use disguises," said Terri. But she was thinking of something else. She had a plan for the perfect revenge on Celia.

"We can get a bunch of disguises from the drama room," said Sonya.

Linda joined them as they walked into class. Terri filled the others in on the plan.

"Who's going to be the fortune teller?" asked Linda.

"Me!" Howard and Terri shouted at once.

"We'll take turns," Terri conceded.

Terri couldn't wait for lunch. When the bell rang she jumped out of her seat and ran ahead of the others to the drama room to ask permission to borrow some things. Then she chose her disguise. She found a safari hat with a see-through veil over the front of it, but Celia would still be able to see who she was. So she wrapped a big scarf around her nose and mouth, and pulled on a flowered skirt that was so long she tripped over the hem. She hardly ever wore skirts anyway, so she really didn't know how to walk in them.

When her friends arrived, they all howled with laughter.

"Terri, that's wild," cried Sonya. "But somebody who moves as fast as you will get killed wearing that long skirt."

She helped Terri roll up the waist of the skirt so she didn't hurt herself.

"You look like you're going on a hunt," said Howard.

"I don't want anyone to recognize me," Terri replied, her voice muffled by the scarf. "As far as you know, I'm Taleeka Star."

"Don't worry about that. Nobody will have any idea who you are," said Howard.

He put on an old coat and man's hat that had been in the closet for ages. Then he pulled the collar up so it hid his face and put on sunglasses.

"You look like a spy," said Sonya, giggling.

Dawn wrapped a scarf around Howard's shoulders. "I don't know whether anyone can trust you, Howard," she said.

Linda and Angela laughed.

"I'm Monsieur X," he said in a funny voice.

"Why not put on this wig and take off that hat," suggested Linda, handing him a curly red wig.

"Now he looks like a cross between a spy and Little Orphan Annie," said Terri, pulling on a pair of white gloves. "But come on. Psychics are supposed to look weird. I don't trust the normal-looking ones. Let's go."

Dawn and Linda pulled a card table and some chairs out of the room while the others chose a spot on the lawn where they would be highly visible.

Terri set herself up at the card table. Linda had brought some different pieces of fabric from the drama room to drape over the tabletop.

"All we need now is a crystal ball," said Linda, who

was quickly making a sign that read, "Psychic Readings—Have Your Fortune Told by Taleeka Star and Monsieur X."

"None of the psychics I've been to have used one," said Terri. "They only go by your birthdate and your age, and a little information about you. After that, they just *feel* who you are."

"Are we going to charge money?" asked Linda.

"I don't think we can just set up a booth and charge money," said Dawn.

"We'll see what kind of response we get, and if it's good, then we can think about asking if we can charge," said Terri.

"We shouldn't hang around the table because then Celia and Polly and Jeannie will figure out who the psychic is," said Sonya.

Angela sent a fifth grader, Amy Garitti, to the lunchroom to tell the students about the psychic's booth. Then Sonya, Dawn, Linda, and Angela hid behind the building so they could see what was going on.

Howard sat down in his disguise and was the first to have his fortune told. "Make it good," he told Terri.

"You will go on a long trip. You will take someone very special with you," droned Terri. "You will be very brave."

"Yeah, right," scoffed Howard. "That's what I did in fifth grade when I went to Africa with my parents. Now tell me what I'll do in the future."

"You'll kill alligators," said Terri in a drony voice like Madame O's. "Then you'll become a great environmentalist and save nature wherever you go."

"That's exactly what I wanted to hear. No accidents or

anything. Here comes Celia and her friends," said Howard. "Thanks for the fortune."

A crowd had gathered. "Where did they come from?" one student asked.

"I don't know, but who cares? I want my fortune told," another student replied excitedly.

Celia nudged Polly. "You go first, Polly."

Polly sat down in front of Terri. Terri started talking in a soft, slow voice, asking Polly when she was born and a little bit about her family.

Then she said: "You are going to meet someone fabulous, tall, blond, and handsome. He's going to take you on a wonderful long trip. In fact, you will meet him while traveling in France. You will have the romance of the century."

Polly squealed with delight. "Tell me more!"

Terri knew that Polly liked to write so she added: "You're going to be a famous reporter and make lots of money. Everyone will know who you are and you'll win a writing prize."

"Which one?" Polly asked excitedly.

"I can't tell," Terri said mysteriously. "But it will be a big one."

Everyone began talking at once. In their curiosity, they pressed closer to the card table.

Polly turned around to her friend. "Did you hear that, Celia?"

"Yes! Get up! Let me go next!" cried Celia, plopping herself down in the seat across from Terri.

Terri held both Celia's hands and gasped. Then she groaned.

"What's wrong?" Celia asked.

"You are doomed," Terri intoned gravely.

"Doomed? What do you mean?" cried Celia, looking worried.

"All your beautiful hair will fall out in clumps," Terri said.

Celia clasped her hands over her head. "Oh, no!"

"And that's not all," said Terri in a deadly tone. "You will be walking along one day and a skateboard will run over you."

"No!" cried Celia, tears filling her eyes.

"Yes, and unfortunately, you will never be the same after that," said Terri.

"Oh, that's so awful!" gasped Celia. "Don't you have anything good to tell me?"

"Yes. You will live a long life," Terri told her.

Celia got up from the chair, looking as if she had just been hit by a skateboard then, thought Terri gleefully. She wanted to tell her lots more horrible things, but then Celia might guess who she was.

Celia was crying, and Polly and Jeannie were trying to comfort her.

"It's just for fun, Celia. She's not a real psychic," said Polly.

"Maybe you should see what that Monsieur X has to say," suggested Jeannie.

"No. I never want my fortune told again as long as I live," Celia mumbled through her tears.

As they were walking away, Terri got up and ran behind the building where her friends were hiding. She pulled off the hat as she ran. When she saw her friends, she burst out laughing.

"Did you see her? She really believed me!" cried Terri. The others hugged her.

"You were great," said Sonya. "I don't think I've ever seen Celia so upset."

"Wouldn't it be funny if she really got hit by a skateboard?" asked Terri, laughing.

"Terri, that is really mean," said Dawn. "And not funny. I think you're going too far with this."

Terri ignored Dawn's comment. She stripped out of her disguise and ran out to see how Howard was doing. But she ran smack into Polly Clinker.

"I saw you take off your hat," said Polly. "You were really nasty to Celia. She really believed you."

"That's not my problem," Terri retorted. "Anyway, she's not exactly an angel, you know." She walked past Polly and back to the card table. Tommy was there, and Howard was telling his fortune.

"You're going to win a prize for an optional in the gymnastics competition," said Howard in a warbly monotone voice. "And, you have a romance in your future. Love will hit you like an eighty-mile-an-hour wind."

Some girls standing nearby started laughing. Tommy turned red. He wouldn't look at Terri or even talk to her, just as he'd promised.

"Listen, I don't want any romance, ever," he said. "Nothing's going to hit me like an eighty-mile-an-hour wind."

"Why don't you tell your own fortune, then?" Howard asked.

Tommy jumped out of his seat and yanked at the wig on Howard's head.

"Howard!" he yelled. "I should've guessed! I'm gonna get you for this!"

Howard stumbled to his feet, knocking over his chair. He raced across the lawn, with Tommy close behind him. As he ran he pulled off his coat, and Tommy nearly fell over it.

Terri's friends gathered around her to watch the spectacle. The boys finally collapsed in a heap on the front lawn. Tommy kept trying to hit Howard, but Howard was fast and kept slipping away and giggling.

Tommy yelled. "This is not funny, Howard, will you shut up? I never want to hear another word about romance, do you hear?"

Howard nodded but he couldn't speak because he was laughing so hard. The crowd of kids that had gathered were whispering, "Romance, romance" under their breaths.

Sonya ran over to Howard and offered her hand. "Let me rescue, kind sir," she said.

Everyone laughed hysterically. Howard turned red this time.

Tommy laughed. "Hey, there's a romance in your future, Monsieur X. Now kiss!" He grabbed a handful of Howard's hair and pushed him toward Sonya.

Howard fell against Sonya and she held on to him so that he didn't fall down. But everyone was whooping and screaming because it looked like they were hugging. They broke away from each other quickly.

"I think I'm going to die of embarrassment," Sonya declared.

"Me, too," said Terri. "I wonder if that's in our future."

Just then, a yard-duty teacher, Mrs. Harris, came over to see what was going on.

"Sonya and Howard were kissing!" cried one student gleefully.

"That's not true!" Sonya insisted.

"All right, the excitement is over now," Mrs. Harris said. "Please return all this stuff to the drama room right away."

The crowd broke up, and everyone ran off in different directions. The girls and Howard folded up the table and chairs and took everything back to the drama room.

For the rest of the afternoon, everyone was chanting, "Romance, romance," whenever they saw Terri, Sonya, Howard, or Tommy.

Terri had to admit that the psychic plan had sort of worked, but it had sort of backfired, too. She wouldn't try it again.

Chapter Nine

On Friday Celia was at her locker, across the hall from Terri's. Tommy walked by and purposely ignored Terri. But the minute Celia saw him, she dropped all her books. Tommy almost tripped on them.

"Oh, no, I'm sorry," she cried, bending to pick up the books.

"Oh, give me a break," Terri muttered under her breath.

"Did you see that?" cried Dawn. "She dropped them on purpose."

"How gross!" cried Angela.

The four girls watched Tommy stoop and pick up the books for her.

"I guess you heard what the psychic said about me," Celia was saying.

"No, I didn't," said Tommy. "But I wouldn't believe in that stuff if I were you."

Celia's face brightened. "Oh, really? You don't think it's real?"

"Nah," Tommy shook his head. "They made it all up." By now, everyone knew that Tommy had exposed Howard as one of the two psychics, but not everyone knew that Taleeka Star was really Terri.

"Well, ever since I saw the psychic I've felt like everything bad was happening to me. But you've made me feel much better." She smiled one of her sicky-sweet smiles.

Terri made a gagging sound. "We shouldn't be standing here watching," she said, turning away. "That's exactly what Celia wants us to do. Plus, she's trying to make Tommy feel sorry for her about the stupid psychic thing. Plus, she wants me to be crying my eyes out about Tommy. And I'm not going to."

She started down the hall to homeroom. Dawn came running up next to her.

"But, Terri, don't you care?" Dawn asked.

"Why should I care?" Terri insisted. "I don't like Tommy, anyway. We used to be friends, but obviously, that was a mistake."

Sonya and Angela caught up with them.

"I'll bet she found out about you being Taleeka Star," said Sonya.

"I don't know. I can't imagine Polly keeping it a secret," said Terri. "But Celia does know Tommy and I aren't speaking to each other ever again. I think I feel like terrorizing Celia," said Terri.

"*I* think you should leave Celia alone," Dawn said. "You know she'll just do something to get back at you."

"Yeah. And maybe you'd better cool it. You're getting almost as bad as she is," Angela said.

"Who asked you, anyway?" Terri demanded angrily. "You're supposed to stick up for *me!* I'm your *friend,* remember?"

"Yes, but it's our duty as friends to tell you when you're getting too bossy and too mean," Sonya said.

"And to tell you when you're wrong," added Dawn.

"Well, I'm going to do it, anyway," Terri declared. She stomped into class, furious with her friends, Tommy, and Celia. Actually, she felt mad at the whole world.

After school, before gymnastics practice, Terri spoke to Robbie Edwards, who was the school's star skateboarder. Robbie didn't like Celia, either, because she always made fun of how short he was. He was a good person to choose because he already had a grudge, thought Terri.

"How about it, Robbie? Will you help me? Just ride really near Celia and scare her half to death," said Terri.

Robbie gave her a funny look. "Really? Why?"

"Because she's expecting it," Terri assured him.

"I'll do it because I can't stand Celia, but are you crazy or what?" asked Robbie, shaking his head.

"No, it's just revenge," Terri said, smiling.

In gymnastics Terri was working on the parallel bars, practicing a full turn. All of a sudden her palms stuck to the wooden bar and a bit of her skin was pulled loose. She was in pain.

"You'll have to wear tape or grips on your hands, Terri, until your palms heal," Ms. Ford told her.

"But I can't hold on good enough with grips," Terri complained. "I guess I have no choice."

She took it a little easier during the rest of class, but she was very impatient about being injured. It would make performing so much harder. Why couldn't everything work out perfectly like it was supposed to?

Later during practice Tommy started to walk toward her as if he were going to talk to her, but she turned away and pretended to be busy. She didn't want to talk to him. She didn't want him feeling sorry for her—even though there wasn't much chance of that.

As soon as she could leave, she went home and practiced on her balance beam. When she asked to skip dinner, her parents got worried.

"Terri, you're working much too hard," her father said. "You've got to take it easier—what have you done to your hands?"

"Just a couple of little blisters," she answered, not completely truthful.

"Well, you know how you are," he said.

"How's that?" she asked, walking over to her trampoline. She jumped while her parents talked.

"You exercise furiously when you're upset about something," her mother pointed out.

"Yeah? Well, how about when I'm upset about a lot of things?" she said.

"Then you exercise even more," said her father. "But you have to learn to talk about your problems. Bottling them up like this isn't good."

"I'm not bottling them up," Terri protested, huffing.

"I'm getting them out." She jumped off the trampoline. "They're all gone."

"Exercising is good, but I think you really need to express what's bothering you in words so we can help. We've noticed that you've been troubled for a while now," said Mrs. Rivera.

"Like since you took me to that stupid psychic and she tried to ruin my life," said Terri. "But don't worry, I went to another one, and now I don't believe the first one anymore."

"How did she try to ruin your life?" asked Mr. Rivera.

Terri told them about what she'd overheard through the closed door. "And I don't believe it, but I think you believe it."

"Well, we don't believe it, either," said Mrs. Rivera. "We have always thought of you as a star." She put her arm around Terri's shoulder.

"But, Mom, you're so involved in all this stuff," Terri cried.

Mrs. Rivera gave her a big squeeze. "Terri, I'm doing research for a documentary about people who are psychic and who claim to have special powers. It doesn't mean that I believe anything they say. Some of them may have gifts and others are complete frauds. But I wouldn't base my life on what any of them say. The same thing goes for astrologers. I'm a reporter. I get my story and I tell it on film. I'm not stating whether psychics are real or not. The audience makes up its own mind. As for me, I thought I might be telepathic and I wanted to learn about that."

"How could you think we'd believe anything a stranger would tell us, Terri?" her father asked. "We know you so

much better than the psychic does. And I thought ¡
how we felt about you.''

"Because you aren't around very much anym   ï
guess,'' said Terri, fiddling with the tape on her palms.
"And when you are around, you're all hung up with your
work or you're doing stuff with Lia. She gets a lot of attention.''

"She does get a lot of attention, but she's little,'' said
Mrs. Rivera. "And you're not around as much as you used
to be, either. You've got your own friends and your own
life. And you don't always like what we plan.''

"I guess we treat you like you're old enough not to need
that kind of attention,'' said Mr. Rivera. "You know, we
ask you to care for your sister, and we treat you more like
an adult.''

"Yeah, I guess sometimes I miss being a kid, though,''
said Terri.

"Maybe you'd like to go out of town with me to an art
show,'' suggested Mr. Rivera.

Terri smiled. "Hey, yeah, that'd be great. After the competition, okay, Dad?''

"Whenever you can fit it into your schedule,'' he said,
smiling.

"Yeah, I see what you mean,'' she said, laughing.

"You might enjoy coming on a shoot with me sometime,
Terri,'' said Mrs. Rivera. "I can always use an extra pair
of hands.''

"That'd be fun, Mom,'' said Terri. Then she remembered something else. "Hey, you're not using that part in
the film about me and Lia, are you? Or that stuff about
romance?''

"Of course not," Mrs. Rivera said. "That was pure nonsense. Just tell me about anything you don't want in the film, and we'll cut it."

Terri felt relieved, as if a weight had just been lifted off her.

"Oh, by the way," Mrs. Rivera said. "Let's get out the family chart that the astrologer finished and take a look at it. Maybe we can learn something from it."

"You're not serious, Mom?" Terri asked.

"No. Just for fun," her mother said quickly. "And for the sake of research."

"The astrologer says that Mondays are great days to buy refrigerators," said Mr. Rivera, and they all laughed.

Chapter Ten

🞧

"I can't believe it!" exclaimed Celia as she strode into gymnastics class on Saturday morning. "Robbie Edwards nearly killed me with his stupid skateboard—just like my fortune said!" She glared at Polly who had come to watch. "And you said the psychic was a farce."

"Well, she is," said Polly. "Look—at Howard."

"You never know. Howard could have some special gift," Celia said. "Now I'm worried about my hair. It's supposed to fall out! I hope it doesn't fall out before the competition." Celia pulled her hair into a ponytail and gasped when a few hairs were left in her hand.

Terri put her hand over her mouth to stop a giggle. Polly was glaring at her. But Polly couldn't prove anything. Robbie's action could have been accidental. But all through gymnastics, Celia was a nervous wreck. She kept losing her balance. Once, she even burst into tears.

Terri couldn't wait until class was over to tell her friends.

She phoned Angela first. "Celia's telling everyone what happened. She's scared to death. And I can't figure out why Polly hasn't told her it was me and not Howard who told her fortune."

"Wow. Maybe Polly's planning something of her own," suggested Angela, whistling. "Anyway, it worked. I wonder what we can do next. Maybe we can put hair remover on Celia's head while she's asleep, and she'll wake up bald."

"Fantastic! Why didn't I think of that?" cried Terri.

"Terri, I was *kidding*," Angela said quickly. "Hair remover is just for mustaches and leg hairs and stuff. You know, the kind of hairs that advertisements call 'unsightly.' To get a whole head of hair off, you'd have to dump gallons of the stuff on. Somehow I don't think Celia would sit still for that."

"Oh, yeah," Terri said. "Well, it would be great if Celia lost all her hair, wouldn't it?"

"Yeah, but that's probably not going to happen until she's about ninety years old," Angela replied.

"I'd like to stay alive to see that day," Terri said, and both girls laughed.

Then Angela stopped laughing. "Hey, Terri, honestly, don't you think you're going a bit overboard with your revenge?"

"No," Terri replied. But this was the second time Angela had brought up this subject. Did she really think Terri was going overboard?

Later, Mrs. Rivera had a commercial to shoot as a favor for a friend of hers. At the last minute, Hildy, Lia's babysitter, called in sick.

"What'll I do?" Mrs. Rivera cried. "I'll have to take

the baby with me, I guess. Terri, could you keep an eye on her for me? It shouldn't take too long, and you both can come over and watch me work.''

''Sure,'' said Terri. Her mom was desperate, and it could be fun.

On the way over to the park where the commercial was to be shot, Mrs. Rivera explained the situation.

''My friend Dotti is doing a commercial for a local car dealership who sells a new kind of car called a Fanfare. The name of the place is Freddie's Fast Cars. She doesn't know what to do because the script is unusable, and they're on a deadline. So I guess we'll wing it. Maybe you can help in some way.''

When they got to the park, the car, a bright red Fanfare, was parked on the lawn in front of some trees.

''Look, Terri. See the car!'' cried Lia excitedly. She squirmed to get out of Terri's grasp.

Terri darted after her sister as she tore across the grass. Mrs. Rivera introduced them to Dotti and the camera crew. Some makeup experts were putting makeup on a man. Terri thought it all looked pretty exciting.

''Terri, please watch Lia closely while I work with the crew,'' Mrs. Rivera requested.

''Sure, Mom,'' replied Terri, taking Lia's hand. Her mother went off to talk with the crew.

Dotti ran a hand through her short blond hair. ''I don't know exactly what we're going to do yet, Terri,'' she said. ''We're just making it up as we go.''

''It'll be fun to watch,'' Terri replied. Watching them, she got a brilliant idea. She ran right over to Dotti.

''Dotti, I've got an idea. Why don't you watch me perform? Maybe you can use me in the commercial,'' she suggested.

"Terri, I'd love to watch, but I'm a little busy just now,'' said Dotti in exasperation. "What do you do, anyway?''

"This.'' With that, Terri twirled onto her hands, then backflipped and leaped across the lawn to stand next to the shiny red car.

Dotti clapped enthusiastically. "Terri, I love it! We won't need much of a script if we have you! Can you do it again? Really, I've got the whole thing now—'You'll flip for a Fanfare!' ''

"Yes! That's perfect!'' Terri cried excitedly. She put Lia on the grass with some toys and told her to stay put. Then she paced off her distance to the car.

She felt a bit nervous because now Dotti really wanted her to do it right. But of course, she reminded herself, she could always perform again if it wasn't perfect.

A group gathered behind the camera, her mom directing them. Terri did the handstand and held it, then went right into the series of backflips and leaps that she had done before. She knew it looked good, but just as she was coming out of her last leap, she smacked something with her foot.

The "something'' let out a howl. Terri looked down to see poor Lia lying on the grass, with blood and tears running down her face.

"Oh, no, Lia!'' Terri cried, bending down to see how badly she was hurt. The baby had a cut lip. She kept crying.

"Terri kicked me,'' she spluttered.

"I didn't mean to kick you, Lia," Terri said. "You got in the way. I'm sorry. Here, let me wipe your mouth."

Terri took the hem of her T-shirt and wiped the blood from Lia's lip, but it kept bleeding. Somebody brought over some ice in a plastic cup which Terri put on her sister's lip.

Just then Mrs. Rivera ran over.

"Oh, Lia, let's look at you," she said, examining the puffy lip. "It looks like she'll need someone to look at that."

Since the pediatrician was off on Saturdays, Mrs. Rivera decided to take Lia to a hospital emergency room.

"Here, I'll take her," offered Dotti's assistant, Russ. He held open the door to his car so everyone could get in.

"What happened, Terri? I thought you were watching her?"

"You saw, Mom. Dotti decided to use me in the commercial."

"But I assumed you'd asked someone to watch her. Oh, never mind. We'll discuss it later." Mrs. Rivera sat with Lia on her lap, and Terri held her sister's hand all the way to the hospital.

Terri stayed with Lia and her mother while Lia had her lip stitched up. Mr. Rivera met them at the hospital. Terri felt really guilty about what had happened, even though it was an accident.

On the way out, she said, "I'm sorry, Mom. I didn't mean for it to happen, you know."

"I know, Terri," Mrs. Rivera said, wrapping an arm around her daughter's shoulder. "It was an accident. But I wish you hadn't just left her alone. Well, maybe if you weren't such a ham, this wouldn't have happened.''

"Oh, yeah! So you do blame me!" Terri cried, stomping ahead. She felt close to tears, but she bit them back.

"Terri, that's not true! I was half teasing," Mrs. Rivera said. "You were excited about what you were doing, and how could you watch Lia and perform at the same time? I don't blame you for what you did. It's mainly my fault. I should have realized you couldn't watch her and perform.''

"Yeah. If you were around more, then maybe it wouldn't have happened," Terri told her mother.

Mrs. Rivera glanced guiltily at her husband and back at Terri.

"Yes. Accidents do happen when people are busy. It's a fact," said Mrs. Rivera.

"Well, I guess being busy and involved runs in the family," said Terri. She realized she was much more like her parents than she had ever thought. She must have inherited her high energy from them.

"What'll happen with the commercial?" Terri wanted to know.

"Oh, they may use it as is, or they'll come up with something else," Mrs. Rivera answered.

Lia was nestled on Terri's lap, holding on to her jacket. She looked funny with her lip all puffy and stitched up.

"She looks like a prizefighter," said Mrs. Rivera.

Terri looked at her sister and smiled. Lia was a neat little kid, even though she was a pest sometimes. Terri really did love her. She stroked her sister's head.

By the time they pulled into their driveway, Lia was asleep in Terri's arms.

Chapter Eleven

❁

On Sunday when Terri got home from horseback riding at Sonya's, there was a package waiting for her.

"Dotti dropped it by. She thought you might be interested," her mom said.

"What is it?" Terri asked.

"I'll never tell," her mom answered, a grin on her face.

Terri ripped open the envelope and tissue paper to find a videotape inside. "Is this what I think it is?" exclaimed Terri. "I wonder if they plan to use my commercial?"

"Don't know. But let's take a look," said Mr. Rivera, joining them.

"Wait, I have to call my friends first," Terri said, rushing to the phone. Within minutes Sonya, Dawn, Angela, and Linda were sitting in the Riveras' living room, waiting for the show to start.

The video rolled. Terri looked fantastic flipping across the lawn. There were more people in the audience than she had realized. The camera cut to a scene of the Fanfare being driven down the road. An announcer said: "You'll flip for a Fanfare!" and then there were people from the audience trying to copy the tricks Terri had done, rolling and falling all over the lawn.

Terri's friends laughed. It looked wonderful.

"Wow, that was great," Angela said.

The phone rang, and Mrs. Rivera answered it. "It's for you," she told Terri.

Terri ran to the phone. "Hi, it's Dotti. I just wanted you to know that 'your' ad is going to run on KATZ-TV, the small independent station in town," she said. "How'd you like it?"

"It was super," said Terri.

"We thought so, too," Dotti said. "And Freddie Fast is really pleased."

"Well, thanks a lot, Dotti."

"You're welcome. And I want an invitation to your gymnastics competition," she said.

Terri promised her a ticket and went back to tell her friends and family what Dotti had said about the commercial's being shown.

"That's fantastic," cried Mrs. Rivera, hugging her daughter. "What a great opportunity for you!"

"I think you should take it to school," said Angela. "And show that piggy Celia a thing or two."

"Yeah!" the other friends agreed.

"I can't wait to see her face when she sees you!" cried Sonya.

"Maybe you should wait until everyone sees the ad on

TV,'' suggested Mr. Rivera. ''It'll probably air next week.''

''Oh, no, Dad,'' Terri exclaimed. ''I can't wait that long. I want to show it to them now. Then they'll know without a doubt that it's me when they see me on TV!''

Terri couldn't wait to get to school the next morning. She marked her tape with a felt pen: ''Terri's Great Commercial.'' She zoomed ahead of her friends, checking every once in a while to see that the videotape was still in her backpack. It was so exciting that she could hardly stay still through the announcements.

Finally, they were over. She raised her hand. ''Ms. Bell, I have an announcement. I brought a tape that's going to be on TV. It's an advertisement for a new car, starring me!''

''Oh, how exciting, Teresa!'' exclaimed Ms. Bell. ''Class, isn't that exciting news?''

The class was already murmuring and whispering. Tommy smiled at Terri as he left the room to run an errand for Ms. Bell.

''We'll watch the tape in a minute, Terri,'' Ms. Bell suggested. ''We have a bit more to do first.''

Terri could barely concentrate on the lesson which Ms. Bell wrote on the blackboard. Celia Forester glared at her, then asked if she could go to the rest room. Ms. Bell gave her permission.

At that moment, Polly tapped Terri on the shoulder.

''Does this mean you're going to be a star?'' Polly asked in a whisper.

"Who knows?" Terri said. "I could get to be a household name."

"Maybe I should ask for your autograph now," said Polly, smiling.

Terri looked at her funny. Polly didn't usually say things like that. She wondered if maybe Celia told Polly to try to get some information from her. She still couldn't believe that Polly hadn't told Celia that she was the psychic.

"I think there's plenty of time for that," said Terri. She thought maybe she should work on signing her name like a famous person, just so she was ready when the time came to sign autographs.

Tommy walked back in and sat down. A couple more students walked in late, and then Celia came back in the room. Just when she was sitting down, Polly tapped Terri on the shoulder again.

"I can't wait to see this video," she said. "Do you have a huge part in it?"

"Well, yeah. Almost the whole video is about me," Terri said proudly.

Celia smiled at Terri. Terri turned around in her seat and put her hand on her videotape. Celia almost started to laugh, and Terri wondered why.

Then it was time to show the videotape. Ms. Bell put the tape in the VCR, and it began to play.

But it wasn't the Fanfare ad. A huge pig filled the TV screen, then he turned his nose to the camera and oinked!

"Hey, there's Terri!" cried Celia delightedly.

The title came on screen, "Pigs—Our Farm Friends."

Terri jumped up. "That's not my tape! Somebody must've taken my tape!" she exclaimed.

By that time the class was in hysterics. The pig was wallowing in the mud, oinking his heart out. Then there were more pigs, all eating or rolling in the mud.

"Look, they're doing gymnastics," said Howard.

Terri gave him a dirty look.

"All right, class," said Ms. Bell sternly. "This is not amusing. Terri's tape is missing. That's what we are here to see. Now anyone who knows anything about her tape, please come forward and tell us!"

Terri stared straight at Celia, because she knew she did it. There was no one else who could do anything that rotten. But Celia didn't move from her seat. Of course, she didn't think she had done anything wrong. She was Ms. Perfect. Except today, she wasn't Ms. Perfect, Terri noticed. She had one lavender ribbon missing from one of her braids, so she looked lopsided.

Even though Terri knew who took the tape, she had to have proof. After class Angela and Sonya waited for her.

"Terri, aren't you coming?" asked Angela.

"Don't wait for me, you guys," she called back. She wanted to snoop around the room to see if Celia had hidden the tape there. As her friends left the room, it occurred to Terri that maybe they had been right about her. Maybe she had been too mean to Celia, and that's why this had happened. *Had* she gotten as bad as Celia?

Tommy came over to her. "Hey, that's great about the video, I mean, it's awful that it got taken. I'm sorry," he said.

"Yeah." Terri sighed.

Everyone hurried out of class, giggling about the pigs.

"Look what I found. Is this yours?" Tommy asked, holding up a lavender ribbon.

"No," said Terri. "But Celia had one in her hair just like it. And she was missing a ribbon! Where'd you find it?"

"Right under your desk," he said.

"That's it! It had to be her." Terri scooped up her books and started for the door. "She must know about me being the psychic, so she's getting back at me! I'm going to the audiovisual room to talk to Mr. Martins."

"Wait for me!" Tommy cried. "I'm coming with you."

They ran out of class and down the hall to the AV room, just in time to see Celia talking to Mr. Martins, the AV instructor.

"Thanks for letting us borrow this," Celia told Mr. Martins, smiling. "The class loved it."

"Glad to hear it was such a hit," Mr. Martins said.

Terri came right up behind Celia and cleared her throat loudly.

"Did you forget something, Celia?" she asked, dangling the lavender ribbon under her nose.

Celia whirled around and looked at the ribbon with horror. "Where'd you get that?" she demanded, snatching it away from Terri.

"It just happened to be under Terri's desk," said Tommy. "I found it."

"We know you took the tape," Terri said. "And I want it back."

"And I know who was the fake psychic who told my fortune," Celia retorted. "That was the worst thing anybody could do."

"No, it wasn't the worst thing," Terri said. "Taking my tape was the worst thing. You deserved getting that fortune, Celia."

Celia turned bright red, reached into her bag and pulled out the tape. She threw it at Terri. Terri caught it.

"I hope *your* hair falls out and you get run over by a speeding train!" Celia yelled. Then she turned and ran out of the room.

"I saw and heard it all," said Mr. Martins, scratching his head. "But what happened?"

Terri explained how Celia had switched her tape for the pig tape, and how important her own tape was. She didn't explain anything about the psychic stuff, however. Fortunately, Mr. Martins didn't ask about it.

"I'll speak to Ms. Bell about this right away," said Mr. Martins.

Terri, Tommy, and Mr. Martins went in to see Ms. Bell.

"I'm so glad you got your tape back, Terri," she said. "I hope we can watch it tomorrow. And I'll call Celia in and speak with her later." Then she wrote out late passes for both Terri and Tommy.

Terri was a little worried that Celia would tell on her for being a "psychic."

Terri tucked her videotape under her arm. She and Tommy walked out of the room together. They had different classes next and took off in opposite directions.

"Hey, Tommy," Terri yelled, turning to him.

He stopped in his tracks and turned around. "Yeah?"

"Thanks a lot—for helping me find this," she said, holding up the tape.

He grinned. "Yeah, sure. You're welcome."

Chapter Twelve

Celia did tell Ms. Bell about Terri being the sidekick, and both girls had to stay after school as punishment.

Over the next week Terri was busy every free second practicing for the competition. By Saturday, the day of the competition, everybody was in high spirits. Terri, Tommy, and Linda were working out together in the gym before the event. Terri felt really good about her warmups—all her muscles were working smoothly. The palms of her hands had healed enough so that she could work on the bars without taping them.

She worked on a ''tumbling pass''—which was a series of tricks all put together. In her floor routine, she had three different tumbling passes.

Tommy was working on the floor. He was doing a back walkover layout. This was two tricks put together—the back walkover was like a backbend except his legs split in the air. Then he did a layout, which was a backward somersault in the air with his body and legs straight.

Linda was practicing a series of turns and handstands on the beam. She wasn't as experienced as either Tommy or Terri, so her tricks were simpler. But Terri could see that she had made a lot of progress.

While Terri spotted Linda, Tommy stood next to her.

"Hey, you know, I'm sorry I didn't talk to you before, Terri," he said.

"It's okay," she replied, concentrating on Linda's turn. "Follow your turn, Linda."

"I just thought you were trying to embarrass me on purpose with that note," he went on.

"I didn't know anything about that note, Tommy," Terri said. "Do you think I'm stupid?"

"No, I just thought . . ."

"Well, Celia wrote that note just to mess things up. Do you think guys are the only people in the whole world who get embarrassed?" she asked him.

"I know you were embarrassed, too," he said. "But I didn't know Celia was causing all the trouble until the videotape. I even thought it was your idea to have that fortune-telling booth."

"It was my idea, but I didn't tell Howard what to say," she said. "I just wanted to get back at Celia."

"Yeah, well, it's okay now," Tommy said, his ears reddening.

"Hey, Linda, you look great!" exclaimed Terri as Linda pirouetted off the beam.

"You do look great," said Tommy.

"Thanks." Linda grinned wide. "I think I've found something I can be really good at."

Ms. Ford had a big van for the whole team to travel in. It wasn't far to the Winchell Auditorium where the competition was to be held.

At the auditorium, the team warmed up for about an hour, in order to get used to the equipment. Then at four o'clock, the performance began.

Different music was played for each team. The Gladstone team walked out first to the music of "Dancing in the Street" and wild cheers from the audience. They stood under a banner of blue and red, their team colors. Terri looked up and saw her friends and family sitting in the bleachers. Lia was jumping up and down, clapping.

Next came the Marcus Elementary team and Wellspring Elementary team, both hot contenders.

The competition began with women's vaulting, uneven parallel bars, men's parallel bars, then women's balance beam, men's pommel horse and horizontal bar, and finally the floor exercises. The Wellspring girls' team went first. Their vaulting performance was fantastic. Wellspring scored very high, and only one person fell.

Then it was Terri's turn. She liked vaulting because it was quick and fun. After watching Wellspring, she was a little nervous, but she breathed deeply. Her stomach growled and she tried to forget that she hadn't eaten. She closed her eyes and concentrated on what she was going to do. Then she saw the head judge give the signal to begin, and Terri gave the same signal back. She was ready.

She did a handspring full twist from the horse, and scored very well.

Linda went after Terri. She was extremely good at vaulting and had great rhythm. She flew through her routine without missing a beat. She didn't score nearly as high as Terri, because her routine was simple. Then came Celia. She did beautifully, too.

Next came the uneven parallel bars for Terri. She did well, her rhythm exactly right. Celia didn't get her hips high enough, and let go of the low bar too early, which made her lose her balance and fall. She looked flustered. If they hadn't been working as a team, Terri would've been pleased that Celia made a mistake.

The Marcus team came next and they did so well on bars that Terri was sure they would win. It was a close match all the way through to the floor exercise.

Terri watched Tommy perform in the boys' parallel bars competition. She was impressed with how well he performed. His rhythm was nearly perfect.

Each student had worked out a floor routine and Terri had to go first. She did her tumbling passes to a bright fast tune—flipping through each trick as if she were born to it. She felt like a human ball as she did a back tuck and then gracefully stretched out to land on her feet. The music ended on a long high note, and Terri pirouetted and bounced to her feet with her hands held high. The crowd went wild.

Celia had chosen a mixture of dance and gymnastics for her routine. The crowd greeted her enthusiastically, and she went into her passes looking as though she were royalty. Her routines weren't really unusual, but she looked so graceful doing them that she earned points.

The other teams each took their turns, and finally it was time for the judges to average up the scores. The teams lined up beneath their banners, waiting. Over the loudspeaker one of the judges announced:

"The winner of the Gladstone County Gymnastics Competition is—Gladstone Elementary School!"

Terri looked around at Linda and Tommy, and they all hugged one another. Even Celia was hugging her teammates. Then Celia grinned at the others and strode forward. She accepted the trophy for all of them and pranced back to her team, acting as if she had won the trophy all by herself.

"She's got a lot of nerve!" hissed Terri.

"It's just like Celia to go ahead and accept the trophy without asking," Linda said huffily.

"Second place goes to Marcus Elementary!" The Marcus team did the same thing, and then came over to congratulate the Gladstone team.

"For the optional floor competition, the winners are: Teresa Rivera, from Gladstone Elementary—first place!"

Terri squealed. Tommy gave her a big hug and she ran out to where the judge stood. He pinned a big blue ribbon on her and handed her a gold trophy.

"Majorine Winamee, from Wellspring Elementary, second place," called the judge. "And Celia Forester, Gladstone Elementary, third place." Tommy had won a second in the boys' competition.

"Hey, smile, Celia," said Tommy as they went up to get their awards.

Celia smiled at her audience and at Tommy. Tommy bowed, accepted his ribbon, and came back to stand next to Terri.

"We really stole the show," said Terri, hugging her trophy.

"You mean, *you* did," Tommy corrected her. "You were great."

"Thanks. So were you," she said, but she felt warmed through by Tommy's words. Terri realized that he was one in a million. He didn't get upset about how competitive she was, or about her winning a first place when he only got a second. Instead, he congratulated her.

They filed out of the auditorium to the dressing area to change clothes. When they had changed, Ms. Ford called them together.

"I'd like you to meet Greta Rensler. She's a talent scout and she's interested in our team."

Greta Rensler was a small blond woman wearing a lavender suit.

"Hi, everyone," said Greta. "I'm really excited about you as a team, and would like to have some of you appear in a television production. And I'll talk to Ms. Ford about setting up a meeting with you later."

Everyone on the team started talking excitedly. The families of the team members came in and joined the group. Terri's and Linda's parents and friends came over to congratulate them.

"Great show, Terri!" her father exclaimed, hugging her. "You were tremendous."

Lia hugged Terri's legs and laughed.

"Terri, it was marvelous," said Mrs. Rivera, handing her a bouquet of roses.

Linda's parents brought their daughter flowers, too. "We're so proud of you," said Mrs. Carmichael, with tears in her eyes.

"I really think Linda would make a great member of the High Visibility Club," Terri said to Angela, Dawn, and Sonya.

"We second the motion," said Dawn. The others agreed enthusiastically.

"Gee, thanks, you guys," said Linda, beaming. "Now I really feel like I belong."

"Let me see your trophy!" cried Lia, reaching for the bright gold trophy.

Terri knelt down to show it to Lia. Lia put it against her mouth and kissed it.

"Pretty," she said.

Terri and her friends laughed. She felt great. Even little Lia liked the trophy. Terri wondered if she could bottle this moment, so she could always feel like this.

Mr. Rivera took a picture of the whole team, with Terri standing next to Tommy and Linda. Later, she would probably look at the picture of the team and remember exactly how she felt at that exciting time. But one thing she felt very certain of—she *was* a winner. It didn't matter what any old psychic said, she thought to herself. Terri Rivera was destined to be great.

About the Author

SUSAN SMITH was born in Great Britain and has lived most of her life in California. She began writing when she was thirteen years old and has authored a number of successful teenage novels, including the *Samantha Slade* series published by Archway Paperbacks. Currently, she lives in Brooklyn with her two children. Both children have provided her with many ideas and observations that she has included in her books. In addition to writing, Ms. Smith enjoys travel, horseback riding, skiing, and swimming.